NEW YORK SCHOOL
OF PERFORMING ARTS

ENROLLMENT FORM

NAME: Louie

SPECIES: Unicorn

INTERESTS: CAKES! And stardom!

DISTINGUISHING FEATURES: Unicorn horn

WHICH CLASSES ARE YOU ATTENDING:

DANCE	✔
DRAMA	✔
SINGING	✔
DIRECTING	✔
PERFORMANCE	✔

EXPERIENCE: Previously typecast as an extremely dashing unicorn in many fairy-tale productions, but now looking for more challenging roles.

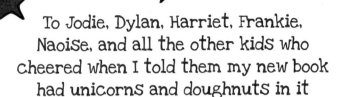

To Jodie, Dylan, Harriet, Frankie,
Naoise, and all the other kids who
cheered when I told them my new book
had unicorns and doughnuts in it

Copyright © 2016 by Rachel Hamilton
Illustrations copyright © 2016 by Oscar Armelles

All rights reserved. Published by Scholastic Inc., 557 Broadway, New York, NY 10012,
Publishers since 1920. SCHOLASTIC and associated logos are trademarks
and/or registered trademarks of Scholastic Inc.

First published in the United Kingdom in 2016 by Oxford University Press,
Great Clarendon Street, Oxford, OX2 6DP.

ISBN 978-1-338-05508-5

10 9 8 7 6 5 4 3 2 1   17 18 19 20 21

Printed in the U.S.A.   23
First Scholastic printing 2017

Photograph on page 91 copyright © 2016 by Stephen Musselwhite
All other photographs copyright © Shutterstock

UNICORN IN NEW YORK

LOUIE
LETS
LOOSE!

RACHEL HAMILTON

Illustrated by Oscar Armelles

SCHOLASTIC INC.

Chapter One

Story Land

Greetings, humans. I am Louie the Unicorn, and this is my tale. That's *tale* with a T-A-L-E. I can't give you my T-A-I-L because I need it for swatting flies and swishing around handsomely.

Anyway, my tale that

is not a tail began with a yawn on
yet another perfect day in Story Land.
The sun had his shiniest hat on, the birds
were belting out their greatest hits, and
the mermaids, goblins, and fairy folk were
living in perfect harmony somewhere over
the rainbow.

I know what you're thinking. Snooze fest!
But then . . .

Excitement arrived with the wind.

I'm talking about the breezy kind of *wind*
here, not the bottom-explosion kind. Mom

says unicorns shouldn't talk about bottom-explosions because we have our sparkly reputations to protect.

So, there I was, with my non-exploding bottom, trotting through the magical forest, when a scrap of paper floated into view.

NEW YORK SCHOOL
OF
PERFORMING ARTS

Are you a magical creature
who loves to perform?
Are you looking for fame and glory?
If so, then we're looking for you!

ENROLL: 4 p.m., MONDAY
BE THERE!

Wow! And another wow!

Fame? Glory? New York? Three times wow!

I'd been desperate to visit New York since I first read about it in the Story Land Library. Bright lights. Big dreams. Even bigger doughnuts. This was my destiny. I, Louie the Unicorn, was going to become a supersized New York superstar.

Nothing could stop me.

Although I should probably check with Mom and Dad first.

Chapter Two

Bye, Mom

"**Why** do you want to leave Story Land, Sugarplum?" Mom asked. "Won't you miss the sunlit meadows and the enchanted waterfalls?"

"Won't you miss the beautiful maidens?" Dad asked, wincing when Mom jabbed him with her horn.

"Meadows make me sneeze, enchanted water gets in your ears, and beautiful maidens only want to talk about handbags and high-heeled hooves," I explained. "I want to go to New York and be a STAR."

"You are a STAR, Snugglebum," Mom said, blowing me a rainbow-sprinkled kiss. "You gave a marvelous performance as the Princess's Dashing Unicorn in the last Story Land Fairy Tale. Everyone said so. Even the dwarves."

"Thanks, Mom, but there's more to acting than being a Dashing Unicorn."

"TROLL POOP!" Dad harrumphed. "There's no 'more' to anything than being a Dashing Unicorn. Just ask the beautiful maidens. Owww!" He groaned as Mom kicked a plate of cupcakes at his head.

Things were not going as planned. No one

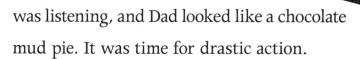

was listening, and Dad looked like a chocolate mud pie. It was time for drastic action.

"If you don't let me go . . ." I paused to let my next words grow bigger. "I WILL BE SAD!"

Dad stopped licking cupcake frosting from his nostrils and stared at me in horror. "Impossible! It is unacceptable for a unicorn to be sad in Story Land."

"Then, from this day forth, I shall be known as Louie the Unacceptably Sad Unicorn."

"Over my dead-yet-still-glorious body! What would the neigh-neighbors think? Help the boy pack, Mother. He'll need glitter, cake, and tap shoes. He's off to New York."

Mom came to the harbor with me the following morning to wave good-bye.

"You're the second departure today." The goblin harbor master consulted his clipboard. "One faun, one unicorn. Never seen it so busy. What's the purpose of your trip?"

I showed him the flyer for the School of Performing Arts. "I'm going to New York to be a star."

He looked back at his clipboard. "No check box for that."

"Just put a check next to 'vacation,'" Mom told him. "My little tootsie pie will be back soon, won't you, darling?" She sniffed as she tucked my legs into the rowboat. "Find your happy place, Louie. And don't forget to write. We'll be waiting for you at the end of the rainbow."

I rowed until Mom was only a dot in the distance and all that remained of my cake stash was a crumb and a chocolate chip.

Darkness fell.

A loud honk woke me. I looked up to see a huge orange ship powering toward my little silver boat. Printed on the side were the words:

STATEN ISLAND FERRY

I uncrossed my legs and used muscles I'd developed during years of ballet training at Little Hooves Dance Studio to leap onto the ferry to New York. In the process, I almost knocked over a small bearded man talking into a large microphone.

Beardy Man pointed to the Statue of Liberty. "The seven spikes on her crown represent the seven seas and seven continents of the world."

"PIXIE PANTS!" I protested, remembering the New York display in Story Land Library. As the ferry arrived in Manhattan, I grabbed the microphone to make a final announcement. "The seven spikes represent the horns of seven celebrated unicorns . . . and, who knows, some day soon, they may add another spike to that crown."

I'm here!!!

12

Chapter Three

Balloons

I bounced through the streets of New York City, feeling very dashing in my new "I ♥ NY" T-shirt. Someone had thoughtfully hung out a line of clothes on their stoop for me to choose from on my arrival. If I had one complaint, it was that everything was a little damp. But I don't want to sound ungrateful.

As I trotted along, unfamiliar odors crept

into my nostrils. My first thought was, *yuck*, but *yuck* is not approved unicorn vocabulary. Neither is *blergh* or *poo-ey*. So, my new-and-improved thought was, *Mmm, what a delicious smell of overheating cars and oniony armpits. Yum.*

Beaming at the natives, I greeted them with my most charming "Tallyho, humans."

The New Yorkers were equally thrilled to see me. Every time I crossed the street, people honked in celebration:

BALLOONS

I recognized this as car-speak for **WELCOME TO NEW YORK, YOU UTTERLY FABULOUS UNICORN, YOU.**

I was touched to see so many drivers shaking their fists to show they wished they could welcome me with tambourines as well as car horns. How charming humans are. Goodness knows how early people must have gotten up to decorate the streets with candy wrappers and empty bottles and potato-chip bags in my honor. It brought a tear of joy to my eye.

As the new unicorn in town, I wasn't sure who to ask for directions to the School of Performing Arts. But then I spotted a man with a "hot dog" cart. Perfect! Who better to ask than a human who had dedicated his life to keeping pets warm? Unfortunately, Hot Dog Man spoke a language I didn't understand.

"Get outta here," he said, giving me a friendly whack on the back.

"Get outta here," he repeated, with a more forceful wallop of affection.

"Get outta here," he bellowed, and this time, his welcoming push knocked me off my hooves.

Worried that his cheery greetings might cause me permanent damage, I gave Hot Dog Man a peck on the

cheek, explained I couldn't stop to chat, and kept going down the road.

Moments later, I noticed a lady with arms full of floating rainbows. She explained these were balloons and they made people happy. What a great invention!

Unfortunately, when I bent to show her my School of Performing Arts flyer, my horn burst a few of the floating balloons of joy.

I stared at the wrinkled rainbows on the floor.

"Balloons don't look like happiness when they stop floating," I told Balloon Lady. "They look more like trash."

Gritting her teeth, Balloon Lady collected the deflated rainbows from the street and spiked them onto my horn. "Better?"

"Yes, indeed. They make magnificent horn decorations!"

Balloon Lady growled.

I stared at her in alarm, beginning to suspect this was no lady, but a troll from Big Bad Mountain in disguise.

I tried to tug off her wig to prove it, but 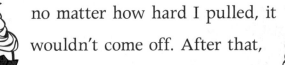 no matter how hard I pulled, it wouldn't come off. After that,

20

things got a little shouty, and it seemed best to keep walking.

Tired and hungry, I wished I hadn't gobbled up all my cakes in the boat. So I did a unicorn jig of joy when I spotted a café at the end of the street.

Chapter Four

Sunshine and Sparkle Dust

I pirouetted into the café and tied a napkin around my neck.

"My compliments, World's Greatest Cupcake Baking Establishment!" I gave the lady who seemed to be the owner my biggest, toothiest smile. "No need for a menu. Bring me everything you've got, please!"

Cake Lady nodded in approval. "Bring out everything we've got for the unicorn!"

It didn't take long before an enormous cake platter arrived. Sunshine and sparkle dust! These cakes were delicious. Cherry cupcakes with vanilla frosting, chocolate cupcakes with white-chocolate sprinkles, strawberry cupcakes piled high with real strawberries, and so many more. Every bite took me a step closer

to cake heaven. My horn shone more brightly. As I finished the plate, Cake Lady and her two waitresses burst into applause. That was when I realized I was the only customer in the café.

"How can a place so magnificent be so empty?" I asked.

Cake Lady stopped clapping and explained, "People are buying their cakes from the big supermarkets because the prices are cheaper."

"Prices?"

"Yes. We charge for quality. So, how will you be paying?" Cake Lady asked with a smile.

"Paying?"

"For the cakes." Cake Lady's smile looked stretchy.

"People in New York have to pay for cakes?"

Cake Lady nodded. Her smile was no longer a smile.

"Um, do you accept glitter as payment?"

The non-smile became a frown.

"Slightly scuffed tap shoes?"

The frown became a scowl.

"What about dead rainbows?" I thrust my balloon-strewn horn at her.

Cake Lady's scowl faded as she pulled the ex-balloons off my horn and stuck her finger through the holes. "I've been trying to make doughnuts, but I can't get the gap in the center right." She gave me a thoughtful look.

"You want to use the balloons?" I asked.

"No." She stared at my forehead. "Not the balloons."

"You want to use my horn?" I realized what she was thinking. "My award-winning horn? You want to stick balls of sugary dough on my award-winning horn?"

She nodded.

"Well, why didn't you say so?" I bowed my head, wondering if my tongue would be long enough to lick off the leftover dough when she'd finished.

Ker-SPLAT! The first doughnut had a hole in it.

Several hundred holes later, Cake Lady agreed I had paid for my cupcakes. She held out her hand and introduced herself. "My name is Victoria Sponge, and this is my café.

Can I interest you in a permanent job? You make a wonderful doughnut-hole-punch. I'd pay you in cake and dollars. Doughnuts will bring in the customers, I'm sure of it."

"Kind lady, that sounds like a simply delicious offer, especially the part where

you mentioned 'cake.' And I would be delighted to bring success to your marvelous establishment. But first I must follow my acting dream." I showed her the flyer for the New York School of Performing Arts. "If I can ever find this school."

"That's easy. It's just around the corner." Victoria Sponge sketched a map on my napkin and pointed at the wall behind me. "There's a poster for their last show."

THE UNICORN OF OZ
STARRING ARNIE
THE UNICORN

They already had a unicorn student at the School for Performing Arts? Sparkle-tastic! This Arnie fellow could be my new best friend.

I rose to my feet and bid Ms. Sponge farewell.

"Good luck, Louie the Unicorn!" she said with a wave. "If your acting dreams don't turn out as you hope, there'll always be a place for you here. Now, take this box of cakes to your new school. You know what they say—cakes make friends."

"Thank you, gracious lady," I said with a bow, and I didn't complain when she used my bent head to poke holes in another five doughnuts.

Chapter Five

Fame School

I followed Victoria Sponge's map to a grand brownstone building.

I knew I'd reached the right place when an admiring crowd gathered around me, chanting "Ahhh! Knee!" It was the first time I'd been celebrated for my leg joints, but this was New York, and my new fans were welcome to admire whatever part of

me they chose. So I waved my knee at the
masses, enjoying the cheers.

The other clue I'd reached the right place was the big sign above the entrance:

WELCOME TO THE NEW YORK SCHOOL OF PERFORMING ARTS

I raised my leg higher and gave the door a kick.

No answer.

I kicked harder.

The door opened, revealing an old fairy with a scowly mouth and stiff wings.

"You ever heard of a doorbell, kid?"

I noticed the bell on the wall. "Terribly sorry. Would it make you feel better if I let you admire my knee?"

"No. It most certainly would not." The fairy turned on her heel and stomped back into the building.

I wasn't sure whether I was supposed to follow, so I stayed where I was and jiggled around a little.

"Hey!" a voice yelled from the crowd outside. "You're not Arnie the Unicorn!"

"No. Indeed," I agreed. "I am Louie the Unicorn."

The crowd groaned.

I'd read about the human habit of using negative words like *wicked* and *sick* to mean positive things. Clearly, groaning worked in a similar way. I bowed and thanked them for their grunt of welcome.

The grumpy old fairy returned, grabbed

my tail, and yanked me inside the building, slamming the door behind us. She bundled me into a room labeled "Principal's Office." It looked like a treasure cave, but without the treasure: dusty and cluttered and full of random shiny things.

"I am the principal." She tapped her wand on the nameplate. "And you are late."

I glanced up at the clock. Five past four. Five minutes late. I'd crossed oceans and time zones, and I was five minutes late.

"Please don't send me away," I begged. "Give me a chance to show what I can do." I dropped my suitcase and cake box and launched into a routine I hoped would knock her magical socks off.

Leaping over her chair with a midair

double-split, I cartwheeled across the desk, walked on my front hooves for a count of ten, and then finished with a daring triple-somersault dismount. It would have been spectacular, except I failed to notice the trash can on the other side of the

 desk and crash-landed into it.

Paper, pencil shavings, and chocolate wrappers exploded across the room. I stood up with my horn jammed in the trash can and a desk lamp stuck on my hoof.

"Ta-da!" I said hopefully.

The principal studied me over the top of her horn-rimmed glasses. As the silence grew louder, I tried a smile and a friendly wave. The movement dislodged the desk lamp, which hit the ground with a bang.

The principal took a deep breath and let

it out very slowly before picking up the lamp and setting it down on the table. Then she handed me a schedule.

"Does this mean . . . ?"

"Yes. You're in. Don't thank me. Thank Arnie the Unicorn. His success opened the door for other mythical creatures and convinced the school board to advertise in Story Land, as well as admitting the normal human intake. But you'll have to work hard. You'll have classes every morning—drama, singing, set design, and then dance with me."

I stared at the schedule, my mind fizzing with excitement. "You're Madame Swirler, the dance teacher?"

She nodded. "You seem surprised. Don't

you think an old fairy can cut it on the dance floor?"

"I am sure you can." I gave her my most dazzling unicorn smile. "If you're the principal, then your lessons must be the best. What kind of dance do you teach?"

"You name it, I teach it: tap, ballet, jazz, disco, hip-hop." Madame Swirler wiggled her grumpy fairy bottom.

I gulped.

"You Story Land kids will have to keep up."

" 'Kids'? Plural? You mean I'm not the only new arrival from Story Land?"

"Four of you showed up." Madam Swirler pointed at three photos pinned on the board behind her. "These are your roommates."

"A mermaid and a faun! New friends!" I

clapped my front hooves together and tried not to worry too much about living with a troll.

Trolls dwelled in the darkest depths of Big Bad Mountain—the only corner of Story Land where the sun didn't shine every day. Unicorns never went there, but creatures that escaped told of a desperate place whose inhabitants were as wild as the thunderstorms that tore through their skies.

I tried to distract myself by asking Madame Swirler, "Will you add my picture to the wall now?"

"We'll see," Madame Swirler replied. "I'm not convinced a country bumpkin like you will last five minutes here."

"I should think not." I liked her confidence in me. "My plan is to stay for at least a semester! One last question," I added. "Could you pull this trash can off my horn now?"

NAME: Miranda

SPECIES: Mermaid

TALENT: Singing. Would like to be an opera star one day.

DISTINGUISHING FEATURES: Lives in a fish tank on wheels

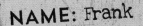

NAME: Frank

SPECIES: Troll

TALENT: Dancing. Has found a leotard that fits, and now nothing will stand in his way.

DISTINGUISHING FEATURES: Slime, muck, and a warty nose

NAME: Danny

SPECIES: Faun

TALENT: Directing. Would like to direct the greats.

DISTINGUISHING FEATURES: Small horns, hairy legs

Chapter Six

Roomies and Rude Burps

"**Afternoon,** roomies!" I entered the dormitory, blinking in surprise when I glanced through the open bathroom door and spotted a large, hairy troll removing a faun's head from the toilet.

"♫ **Hello-o-o-o-o** ♫," sang the mermaid in the corner. "I'm Miranda. That's

42

Frank. And the guy with his head stuck down the toilet is Danny. He tripped."

"I see," I said, although I wasn't sure I did. "I like your posters."

Miranda had decorated the walls around her tank with huge audience photos, taken from the stage at New York's Madison

Square Garden. It made it look like she was performing to a crowd.

"Have you been there?" I asked.

"No," she admitted. "But I've promised

myself I'll perform there one day. It's why I came to New York. I want to use my voice to make the world a happier place."

Miranda propped herself up in her tank to brush her hair. She growled when the silver brush got stuck in her curls and one of its teeth broke. "Grrrr. Tangles. Frank, when you've finished pulling Danny out of the toilet, can I borrow your comb?"

Frank? She was asking Frank the Troll from Big Bad Mountain for a comb? Why would a warty mountain monster have hair-styling equipment?

I've never been to Big Bad Mountain, but everyone knows it's full of big bad meanies. So when Frank emerged from the bathroom, reaching into his pocket, I took a step backward.

But all he pulled out was a comb.

As he moved toward the tank, I lowered my head, ready to charge to the beautiful mermaid's rescue if necessary. Because that's what we dashing unicorns do. Luckily, my services weren't required.

"Are you sure you're from Big Bad Mountain, Frank?" I asked as he gently combed Miranda's hair. "I thought you had to be an evil monster to live there."

"Nope," said Frank. "You just have to be a monster. Evil is optional."

"I didn't know that."

"We don't tell many people. It keeps out the tourists. Besides, most monsters choose evil." Frank picked his nose, looked embarrassed, wiped it on his pants, and continued combing Miranda's hair.

A soggy faun emerged from the bathroom, shaking the water from his body. He pulled his wet shirt off and hung it on my horn.

"Um . . . Hello!" I greeted him. "You must be Danny. Are we playing dress-up?"

"Oh, sorry! I thought you were a clothing rack," Danny said.

"A clothing rack?" I spluttered. "This horn has won awards."

"Horn? What horn?"

I studied Danny, wondering if he might be crazy. "The horn on my head."

"Horses don't have horns."

"Horses?" I screeched. "Sir, I am no horse. I am a unicorn."

"Ah, sorry. I lost my glasses on the way here, and without them I can't see past the nose on my face. Anyway, s'nice to meet you." Danny reached out and shook my ear.

"Um. Nice to meet you, too."

"B-u-u-u-rrrrrrrrrrrrrrrrp." Frank's belch rattled the room and sent water splashing out of Miranda's tank. He blushed tomato-red.

"Sorry!" he said. "I'm trying to control my troll urges as part of my training to be a dancer. But it's not going so well."

"A dancer?"

Frank nodded and showed me his leotard.

48

"I've been practicing my flower dance. Want to see?"

"Of course he does. Everybody loves the flower dance," Miranda crooned. "♫ **Come on Frank-e-e-e. Be the se-e-eeed.** ♫"

There was something hypnotic about Miranda's voice, and Frank instantly curled up into a tiny ball. He looked awkward at the start, but after a minute or two, Frank WAS the seed.

"♫ **Be the ro-o-ooot, Frank-e-e-e** ♫"

Frank was the root, searching for water and nutrients.

"♫ **Be the le-e-eeaf, Frank-e-e-e** ♫"

Frank was the leaf.

Frank was the bud.

Frank was the . . .

"DINNER!" roared Frank as the smell of mac 'n' cheese drifted into the room. Frank was no longer a flower—he was a troll on a dinner mission. He grabbed Miranda's tank and charged out of the dorm.

"Wow!" I said, watching them go.

"Owww!" Danny replied, walking into a potted plant.

"Take my horn," I told him. "I'll lead you to dinner."

"Thanks." Danny frowned all the way to the dining hall, pausing for extra frowning every time he bumped into something. "How can I become the world's greatest director if I can't even see what's in front of me?"

"Good question," I replied helpfully.

Chapter Seven

Dashing Unicorns

The dining hall was full of tables, chairs, and lots of shouty humans. But everyone stopped shouting and started staring when Danny and I walked in. You'd think they'd never seen a nearsighted faun being guided by a unicorn before.

Danny let go of my horn and walked into the nearest table. Mac 'n' cheese flew everywhere. The other students didn't look happy.

"Howdy, humans!" I yelled, confident a unicorn joke would cheer people up and save Danny from being pelted with macaroni. "What do you call a unicorn's dad?"

No one spoke.

"POP corn. Ha! Get it?"

I'm sure the cafeteria lady doling out the dinner laughed (although it might have been a sneeze), so I pressed on. But before I could make my next hilarious joke, the dining hall's sound system crackled into action with a funky tune. ♫ **Simply the Best** ♫ played over the speakers, and everyone cheered and whooped. They'd given me a theme song! How wonderful.

"Thank you. Thank you, all," I shouted over the music.

"Get out of the way!" a small girl with a big voice yelled. "You're blocking the view."

"Yeah. Move. We can't see," agreed a boy wearing an "Arnie's Army" T-shirt.

I turned to find out what everyone was looking at and recognized the long, handsome face from the *Unicorn of Oz* poster.

Arnie the Unicorn!

Arnie strutted the length of the dining hall in time with the music. It was obvious from his killer moves that Arnie was the kind of unicorn Dad would describe as Dashing-with-a-capital-D. It was also obvious from his flaring nostrils that Arnie was angry.

"How DARE you talk over my intro

music?" he harrumphed, stalking over. "No one talks over Arnie's intro music."

"Lovely to meet you, Arnie." I beamed with delight. "I'm Louie, and I just know we're going to become the best of friends."

"Friends?" Arnie stamped his hoof. "Pah! There is only room for one unicorn in this school . . ."

"That's a shame," I said. "We've only just started getting to know each other. When are you leaving?"

"Not me, you uni-fool," Arnie said. "You are the one unicorn too many. I am Arnie the Unicorn. You are no better than a donkey with a stuck-on horn."

"A donkey? Ha." I realized Arnie was looking for a comedy partner, and I joined

in. "What do you call a donkey with three legs?"

"Idiot!"

"No, silly. A wonkey!"

Arnie dumped a bowl of Jell-O on my head.

Holy cow! Arnie was putting everything into this show. I joined in with his clowning by shaking my head and splattering him with Jell-O. "JELL-O!" roared Frank, from the other side of the room, sniffing the air. He powered across the dining hall, leaped on me, and started licking my face.

"Ugh! Stop!" I protested, trying to wriggle free. "There can't be any more Jell-O left, Frank. STOP LICKING!"

"Sorry!" Frank let go and stared at his hairy feet in shame. "It's hard to suppress my Jell-O urges."

"Jell-O? Seriously? I thought trolls ate kittens and babies." I remembered my earlier glimpse of Frank's baby-shaped lunch box.

"Not this troll." Frank licked his lips and eyeballed Arnie's Jell-O–splattered mane. "THIS TROLL LOVES JELL-O!"

"I'd run if I were you, Arnie," I warned.

Arnie narrowed his eyes at me. "You think you can get rid of me just like that? You think you can waltz in here and be number one unicorn?"

"No. I just thought you'd prefer not to be licked by Frank."

"Ugh." Arnie shuddered, backing away. "Don't let that disgusting beast anywhere near me."

"He's not a beast," Miranda shrilled. "He's Frank, and he's fantastic. Move me closer to that rude unicorn!" she ordered Danny.

"Rude? *Moi?*" Arnie protested. "How DARE you criticize my manners, you . . . you . . . sea monster!"

"She's a mermaid, not a monster." Danny stumbled forward. "Have you lost your glasses, too, Arnie? Tough, isn't it? Can I get your autograph? I'm a big fan. I'd love to direct you one day."

"I don't need glasses," Arnie neighed indignantly. "Arnie the Unicorn has perfect vision—and what I see is a second-rate unicorn, a stinky troll, a moldy sea monster, and a blind goat boy. I don't know what this school's coming to."

"♩ Hey, Lo-o-ooouie ♩" Miranda sang. "♩ Where do you put a rude unicorn? ♩"

"Oooh, I know this joke." I clapped in delight. "In the naughty uni-corner!"

Arnie scowled and clomped off, kicking Danny the Faun out of his way as he joined the kids wearing "Arnie's Army" T-shirts. They cheered and fist/hoof-bumped him.

Frank helped Danny up, dusted him off, and set him back on his feet.

"Thanks, Frank," Danny said.

"What are friends for?" Frank put one huge rocklike hand on Danny's arm and patted Miranda's tank fondly with the other one. "Thanks for defending me, Miranda."

"Don't mention it." Miranda stared across the dining hall to where Arnie was now reciting poetry to his fans. "We haven't seen the last of him, you know."

"I hope not," I said cheerily. "I'm looking forward to us becoming the best of friends."

"I admire your optimism," Danny told a stack of dirty dinner trays beside me.

Poor faun. Later that night, as I showed Danny how to brush his teeth instead of his eyebrows, I promised myself I'd find a way to help him see again.

Chapter Eight

Shakespeare and Squashed Toes

During drama class, we learned auditions would be held at the end of the week for this semester's school musical, *The Unicorn and the Chocolate Factory*.

I cheered. "The main part has my name written all over it!"

"Nuh uh!" A blond girl in an "Arnie's Army" sweatshirt shook her head. "Arnie was amazing in *The Unicorn of Oz,* and *The Unicorn, the Witch, and the Wardrobe.* You don't stand a chance."

"We'll see. May the best unicorn win!"

"Oh, he will." Arnie's Army Girl tossed her hair over her shoulder and sashayed to the other side of the gym as Mr. Curtains, our small, bearded drama teacher, signaled for everyone to sit.

I listened, entranced, as he explained that every new student would perform a song or speech of their choice in front of the rest of the school to introduce themselves.

This was the perfect opportunity to show how magnificent I'd be in *The Unicorn and the Chocolate Factory* before the official auditions.

I knew a few lines from Shakespeare, who seemed to be humans' favorite poet and playwright, so when it was my turn to move to the front of the gym, I decided to impress the drama teacher by performing a scene from the play *Romeo and Juliet*.

"But soft! What light through yonder window breaks?" I began.

"♪ **Ooh!** ♪" Miranda wailed musically. "Who's breaking windows? What if they break my tank?"

"Shush," I hissed. "Shakespeare won't break your tank, I promise. Can I keep going now?"

Miranda nodded.

"It is the east, and Juliet is the sun.

Arise, fair sun, and kill the envious moon."

"♪ **Nooo** ♪" Miranda clutched her chest.

"First they're breaking glass. Now they're killing people."

"Stop it! No one's killing anyone. It's just a play. It's a beautifully written . . . Oof!" I grunted as Danny moved forward for a better view and crashed into me, slamming

me against Miranda's tank and sploshing water over the audience.

"Sorry. Disaster!" I backed away as the water came out in waves. "Uh-oh. My fault. Sorry."

"Owww!" Mr. Curtains bellowed when I took one backward step too many and crushed his toes.

"Argh! Accident! Sorry, Mr. Curtains. Sorry, Miranda. Sorry, everybody." I kept apologizing until the drama teacher had been carried off to the nurse's office and the janitor had refilled Miranda's tank.

"It's not all bad, Louie," Frank reassured me, scratching his armpit and pulling out a flea. "Mr. Curtains seemed impressed by the Shakespeare, until you crushed him."

Out of the corner of my eye, I spotted Arnie approaching, with a strange smile on his handsome face. He put a hoof around me conspiratorially and led me to a quiet corner.

"Louie, my friend, do not be downhearted. This little speech isn't important. It's the audition that counts. You just have to make sure you are in the right place at the right time. Would you like me to draw you a map to the audition hall?"

"Yes, please!" I felt better already. Arnie had called me his friend. It wouldn't be long before we were best buddies.

Chapter Nine

Badly Drawn Maps

Things were going wonderfully well at the School of Performing Arts. I know teachers aren't supposed to have favorite students, but I could tell Madame Swirler liked me. She had this funny habit of scrunching up her face whenever she saw me, and she was always playing games. Her favorite was hide-and-seek. Yesterday, when I popped into her office, I spotted her hiding behind the lampshade, so I won! I told her I was looking forward to playing more hide-and-seek and having some nice long chats with her soon. She pulled another scrunchy face.

Frank was a big success, too. Everyone was amazed by his dance skills, if not his personal hygiene. And no one could resist Miranda's magical voice.

But things were tougher for Danny. He was top of the class for set design because our teacher, Madame La Stage, let us read the information to him and jot down his answers. But everything else was a struggle.

Dance was particularly tricky, and in our second lesson with Madame Swirler, Danny danced right out of the window. Fortunately for Danny, Mr. Curtains was walking under the window at the time. He was moving slowly due to his injured toe, so he made a soft, comfy landing for Danny, who was able to escape with only a bruised bottom. Mr. Curtains wasn't so lucky, but on the positive side, he forgot about his sore foot.

To everyone's relief, Mr. Curtains felt much better by the morning of the auditions. The hallways were buzzing with our excitement, and my heart was pounding. I'd done everything I could—learned my piece by

heart, practiced in front of the mirror, performed breathing exercises, polished my horn—but I was still nervous. I told my friends to go on ahead while I did a few stress-relieving shakeouts.

"What if you can't find the audition hall?" Miranda worried.

"Don't worry. I have Arnie's map. What could possibly go wrong?"

Twenty minutes later, after sending me down countless dark corridors, Arnie's map led me to the boiler room in the basement of the school.

I must have misread the map while I was concentrating on my audition lines. I set off again, yelling my first line, "Greetings,

Oompa Loompas," as I made my way toward the *The Unicorn and the Chocolate Factory* auditions. Hooray! This looked more like it. I turned the final corner . . . and found myself back at the boiler room. Hmmph.

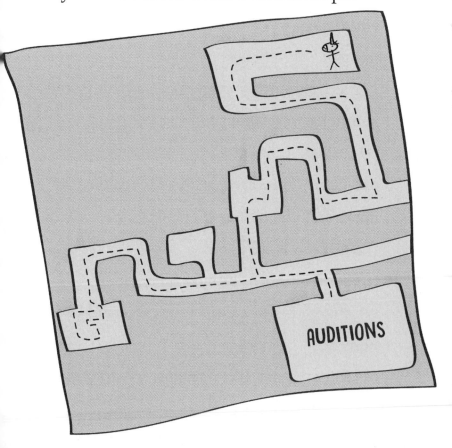

Third time's a charm. I charged off, but I got lost in the maze of corridors and ended up . . . you guessed it . . . in the boiler room. The door slammed behind me, making me jump. A breeze in the basement? I tried the handle.

Stuck.

The time on the cracked clock suggested auditions were about to start.

I yelled, I hollered, I whinnied, but no one came. I lowered my head, steadied my horn, and charged at the door.

OWWWWWW!

Door beat horn. It must be made of steel.

I charged. I kicked. I charged again. Still no luck.

After what felt like decades, but according

to the clock was less than an hour, someone heard my distress, and the door swung open.

"Madame Swirler! My hero! My savior! I love you, I love you, I love you."

Madame Swirler glared at me. "Well, I don't love you, you silly unicorn. What are you doing making all this noise beneath my office? Look what you've done to the door."

"Look what the door's done to me," I protested, showing her a scuffed hoof. "I'd love to stay and chat, Madame Swirler, but I have to get to the auditions! I was born to be the unicorn in the chocolate factory!"

"Born to be the hooligan in the boiler room, I'd say," Madame Swirler grumbled. "You're too late for the auditions. They finished ten minutes ago."

"Noooo!" I shook my head violently, dislodging an enormous cobweb.

"Yes." Madame Swirler pushed me toward the door. "I'll show you. Follow me. We don't want you damaging any more school property."

I continued shaking my head as she led me up the stairs, toward the audition hall. I couldn't believe they hadn't waited for me.

But Madame Swirler was right—I was too late. When I burst into the room, people were lifting Arnie in the air and congratulating him on the lead role.

I looked at Arnie and then down at my map. My bottom lip wobbled. I decided I must be cold and moved closer to the radiator.

A boy with a cardboard horn attached to his forehead pushed past me to get closer to his hero. "Arnie, that speech from Shakespeare was fantastic," he declared earnestly.

"Yeah?" Frank growled, studying a booger on his finger. "Almost as fantastic as when Louie did it on Monday."

I didn't want to see what Frank planned

to do with his booger, so I scanned the room for my other friends. Miranda was in the corner, comforting Danny.

"♫ Lo-o-o-ouie ♫" she warbled. "We tried to delay auditions, but some people wouldn't let us." She glared at Arnie's Army. "Where have you been?"

"Stuck in a boiler room." I shook the cobwebs from my horn and accidentally swallowed a spider. "What's wrong with Danny?"

"He asked Arnie for an autograph," Frank replied, eating his troll-booger.

"Yuck. So . . . ?"

"He asked the wrong end of Arnie."

I giggled at the thought of Danny talking

to Arnie's bottom. We really needed to get Danny some glasses.

Frank nodded. "Arnie went crazy when everyone laughed. He told Danny he'd never direct in this school."

"He said he wouldn't allow 'sea monsters' in his musicals, either." Miranda glowered at Arnie as he trotted over.

"Seems the best unicorn won," Arnie declared, watching me pull a spider's leg out from between my teeth.

I felt like I'd been kicked in the horn. Must have been all that charging at doors. "Maybe you're right." I nodded sadly. Arnie was looking particularly dashing and cobweb-free.

"No," Danny said, glaring in the vague

direction of Arnie. "YOU are the best unicorn, Louie! You are kind. You are honest. You don't threaten people. And you don't cheat."

"How DARE you!" Arnie swished his mane in indignation.

"Danny!" I gasped. "Unicorns never cheat. Friend Arnie, congratulations on your role. I'm sure you'll be magnificent. Perhaps I'll get my chance another time."

"You'd be so lucky," Arnie retorted.

"Thank you." I smiled. "I think I will."

I turned to my gloomy-looking friends. "Buck up, roomies. I have the perfect happy place for us." I pulled out the Sunshine Sparkle Dust Café napkin I'd been saving. "Look! Victoria Sponge created a real-life treasure map. If we follow the route backward, it'll lead us to the best cupcakes in the world."

"Hey, Arnie," I added, "she could give you map-drawing lessons, too. Let's go, everyone! Happiness awaits."

Chapter Ten

Doughnut Holes

Arnie couldn't come with us to the café because he was busy washing his mane. So Frank, Miranda, Danny, and I visited the Sunshine Sparkle Dust Café without him. We admired the display of delicious cupcakes. Saliva dripped from Frank's chin onto his furry feet.

"Hello again!" I waved at Victoria Sponge. "I have come to offer you my doughnut-poking services in exchange for as much cake as it takes to make a faun, a troll, and a mermaid happy."

We were the only customers, so she showed us to the best seats, beside the window, and I set to work. I soon had an efficient system going. Ker-SPLAT! Ker-SPLAT!

I worked hard. Cheering up my friends was taking a lot of cake.

"How can I direct if I can't see?"

Danny stared into space . . . or perhaps at his caramel cupcake . . . it was hard to tell.

"♩ Will I ever get my chance to si-i-iiing in front of a crowd? ♩"

Miranda serenaded her tenth chocolate doughnut.

"Don't be sad," I told them. "At least we'll always have the Sunshine Sparkle Dust Café."

"Actually, that might not be true." Victoria Sponge helped herself to three more doughnut balls. "I have two weeks left on the lease. If I can't get more people to buy my delicious cupcakes and doughnuts, I'll have to close for good."

"No!" I cried. "We can't let that happen. We need a plan!"

"B-u-u-rrrrrrrrrrrrrrrrp," replied Frank.

I closed my eyes to avoid the sight of Frank's mouth overflowing with cheesecake, and I tried to come up with café-saving ideas.

"Eureka! I have a plan. And it doesn't involve belching." I gave Frank a stern look. "WE WILL PUT ON OUR OWN SHOW! It will be cake-themed, we'll do it here in Sunshine Sparkle Dust Café, and everyone will get their wish. Miranda will sing in front of a crowd. Frank will dance or burp or do whatever makes him happy. Victoria Sponge will sell cakes to the people who flock to see us. Danny will show everyone what a great director he is. And we'll raise enough money to buy him a pair of glasses."

Everyone cheered.

Together we worked out the running order of the show. Danny had a surprisingly clear vision of how everything would work. Miranda would open by bursting out of a giant cake, singing an operatic mash-up of ♫ **Hot Cross Buns** ♫ and ♫ **If You're Happy and You Know It** ♫.

Frank would channel his expressive dance talents into a soulful performance of ♫ Run, Run as Fast as You Can, You Can't Catch Me, I'm the Gingerbread Man ♫. I would follow with a fast-paced dance number to ♫ Do You know the Muffin Man? ♫. Then we would all come together in a spectacular theatrical rendition of ♫ New York, New York ♫.

It was going to be fabulous!

With that arranged, we made posters. Admittedly, Miranda's were soggy, Frank's were slimy, and Danny drew on the table rather than on the poster paper, but the thought was there. We stuck them all over town.

Arnie's Army followed us everywhere,

removing the posters as soon as we put them up. I thanked them for their hard work, because it turned into a game everyone could play—moving posters from one location to another and seeing who could find the funniest places to post them.

It was lots of fun until someone stuck one on Madame Swirler. The game ended quickly after that.

Everything was going perfectly until the day I came to rehearsals at the Sunshine Sparkle Dust Café and found Danny forcing Frank into Miranda's tank.

"You need water," Danny was insisting. "Without it you'll die."

Frank looked confused, but we'd all

gotten used to following Danny's directions, so he allowed himself to be squished into the tank.

Miranda, who'd been asleep, was alarmed to find an intruder inside her tank and whacked Frank with her tail. Her intruder strategy was clearly attack first, ask questions later. Luckily, Frank the Troll turned out to be surprisingly agile under water and wiggled back and forth, somersaulting around her tail to save himself.

"Stop it!" he said when he surfaced, gulping for air before Miranda knocked him back below the water. "S'me!" *Gulp.* "Frank!" *Gulp.* "Get." *Gulp.* "Off." *Gulp.* **"B-u-u-rrrrrrrrrrrrp."**

"Frank?" Miranda stopped splashing and grabbed his head. "What are you doing in my tank?"

"Danny shoved him in," I told her. "I think he mistook him for you."

"♪I nearly drowned Frank♪," Miranda wailed.

"No." Danny sighed. "I nearly drowned Frank."

"Cheer up." I passed them both a doughnut. "Nobody drowned anybody, and now we know how good Frank looks in the water. We can build it into our show with an underwater acrobatic display for our "New York, New York" finale. It'll be perfect!"

"I can't go on like this." Danny hadn't touched his doughnut. He was in a bad way.

"Worry not." I pushed the doughnut into his mouth. "The show is in ten days, and we'll use some of the profits to buy you new glasses. You'll see! Ha, see what I did there?"

Danny groaned but managed to swallow his doughnut.

Chapter Eleven

The Vegetable Aisle

The big day finally arrived.

"It's showtime!" Miranda gazed across the Sunshine Sparkle Dust Café with shiny eyes and an even shinier dress.

"It's showtime!" Danny declared to a mop bucket.

"B-u-u-rrrrrrrrrrrrp." Frank belched and stroked his hairy belly. "If it's showtime, where is everyone?"

I looked at the party tables sprinkled with edible confetti, at the banners made from brightly colored cupcake wrappers, at the helium balloons in the shape of sprinkle-covered doughnuts . . . and at the complete lack of audience.

The only people in the café not appearing in the show were Victoria Sponge and her waitresses, who had dressed up like human cupcakes with cherry hats on top. They stood behind their cupcake-decorating stations, and awaited the rush of guests. So where were those guests?

"Maybe no one's bothered to come see the show," Danny suggested miserably.

"Goblin garbage!" I declared. "Everyone wants to see our show. It has us in it. There has to be another explanation."

I poked my head outside to investigate. "Uh-oh!"

"Uh-oh?"

"I might know where everyone is." I waited until my friends joined me on the pavement and then pointed across the street. The opposite wall was plastered with defaced posters saying we'd moved our show to the vegetable aisle of the local supermarket.

"ARNIE!" roared Frank. "I'll rip that unicorn limb from limb."

"Control your urges." Miranda put a calming hand on Frank's arm. "♩ Be the se-e-eeed ♩."

Frank shook off her hand and explained, rather forcefully, that he did not want to be the seed.

"Relax, Frank," I said. "If, indeed, this is Arnie's handiwork, he's done us another favor. There will be zillions of people in the supermarket vegetable aisle. I simply have to go to them and lead them here. We'll have a full house!"

Chapter Twelve

A Cake-Loving Conga

I t was after four o'clock before I returned to the Sunshine Sparkle Dust Café. I had to wait for the people in the vegetable aisle to pay for their broccoli and carrots before they'd let me lead them, conga-style, through the streets of New York.

Excitement built as we danced our way through the city. Taxis honked and children waved as more and more people joined the

party. The closer we got to the café, the louder and more energized the throng of cake-lovers became.

I had a flicker of panic when I saw the lights were off in the café. But I breathed again as I spotted Miranda's silhouette in the window. They hadn't given up on me yet.

I bounced in. "Do not fear. We are here!"

Frank was first to recover from the shock of seeing a huge conga parade through the café door. He turned the lights back on, yelling, "Surprise!" to make it feel like a party.

I spotted Arnie and Madame Swirler sneaking in the back door and gave them an exuberant wave. They both pulled scrunchy faces.

We'd cleared the tables to the sides of the café, so our new friends settled into the doughnut-shaped beanbags scattered across the floor and started munching on sugar-coated goodness. Frank and I removed the temporary curtain and revealed the stage we'd created on the cake counter. When everyone was settled, we dimmed the lights. Miranda burst from the fake cake we'd built around her tank and began to sing.

After she'd finished her ♫ **Hot Cross Buns/If You're Happy and You Know It** ♫ medley, everyone's eyes were damp . . . and not only because Miranda had soaked them all with her extravagant dance moves.

Frank was next. He WAS the little old

woman and the little old man and the runaway gingerbread man and the sly fox in ♫ **Run, Run as Fast as You Can, You Can't Catch Me, I'm the Gingerbread Man** ♫. The audience adored him.

Then it was my turn.

♫ **Do You Know the Muffin Man?** ♫ brought the house down—not to mention a few lampshades and a small chunk of ceiling when I finished my dramatized search for that missing man of muffins with a back handspring. Arnie moved nearer the counter-slash-stage during my piece, watching me closely. I grinned and gave him a hoofy wave as I sprang out of my encore backflip.

By the time Frank dived into the tank for

our ♫ **New York, New York** ♫ finale, people were cheering, whooping, banging their broccoli on the tables, and tossing coins into the collection cookie jar.

I stamped my hooves in time with the music until everyone was on their feet, clapping to the rhythm of "New York, New York." Arnie continued edging forward until he was in prime position to see my final jump. As I began my run up to vault back onto the counter, Arnie gave one of his odd smiles and put his hoof out for a high five. It was only as I galloped forward at top speed that I realized Arnie had misjudged the height of the high five, and he was going to accidentally make me trip!

I went flying horn-first into the audience.

I saw the panic on people's faces and knew I had to do something, fast. Calling on all my acrobatic skills, I twisted in the air, passing only inches above the heads of the audience. I used the momentum to launch into a magnificent midair pirouette.

The crowd went wild. Squealing, stamping, cheering, and crying out for more. It was an incredible feeling. I couldn't wipe the smile from my face as Victoria Sponge climbed on stage, thanked us for the performance, and asked the crowd for donations.

I ran to congratulate my friends. Sadly, I couldn't thank Arnie for his help because he was already galloping out the door, on his way to perform other good deeds elsewhere, no doubt.

"I wish I could have seen your acrobatics, Louie," Danny said wistfully. "Sounds like you were amazing." He reached out and fist-bumped a cake stand.

Miranda, Frank, and I looked at one another.

"Glasses," we said in unison.

Chapter Thirteen

Glasses

After the cheering crowds had gone, Victoria Sponge danced around her cash register and declared that the Sunshine Sparkle Dust Café would be able to continue creating the best cupcakes in the world. Delighted, we counted the coins in the cookie collecting jar. Twenty cents, fifty cents, a dollar. In total we had $2.99.

The waitresses weren't sure it would be

enough to buy Danny a pair of glasses. But it had to be.

Outside the café, the night market had begun. I wandered among the street sellers until I found the perfect glasses. Made of thick tortoiseshell plastic, they went up at the corners in a way that would make Danny look distinguished and creative. I loved them. The only problem was the price—$5.

"Would you take $2.99?"

"Nope," said the salesman. "Five dollars. Best price you'll get. Now move out the way,

you're blocking my real customers. Sir, Madam, how can I help you?"

"What if I put on a show for you? I'm a performing unicorn. Your customers will love it."

"My customers don't want a show." The salesman pushed me to one side and handed over a pair of glasses in exchange for a five-dollar bill from the young couple. "If you insist on prancing around, I'll charge you ten dollars for the glasses."

"Perhaps a few unicorn jokes instead?" I suggested. "Here's one—what do you call unicorn dandruff?"

The salesman ignored me and passed a pair of gold aviator glasses to the man standing behind me.

I poked the salesman with my horn. "Corn flakes. Get it? Here's another one. What's the difference between a unicorn and a carrot?"

The salesman let out a big sigh. "Son, if

I give you these glasses for $2.99, will you go away?"

"I'm afraid so. I want to give them to Danny as soon as possible."

"In that case, they're yours." The salesman thrust the glasses at me and snatched my money.

"You are a wonderful man. Let me thank you with more jokes."

"No." The salesman gave me a shove. "Really. No. More. Jokes. Take the glasses and GO!"

I galloped back to the café and handed the glasses to Danny with a flourish.

"For me?" he asked, putting the glasses carefully on his face.

I nodded, and for the first time since I'd

known Danny, I didn't have to follow up my nod by telling him I'd nodded.

"I CAN SEE!" Danny gave me a big hug. "You are the best unicorn in the world! You're worth ten Arnies."

Victoria Sponge reached across and ruffled my mane. "You saved my business. I'd make that twenty Arnies."

"♩A hundred♩," sang Miranda.

"B-u-u-rrrrrrrrrp," said Frank the Troll, which I took to mean I was worth about a thousand Arnies.

Chapter Fourteen

Spilled Milk

I was still full of show-related smiles the following day. So it wasn't as hard as I'd expected to be in the audience rather than on stage for *The Unicorn and the Chocolate Factory*.

Arnie was wonderful. I was the first to get to my feet for a standing ovation, confident he'd do the same for me when I was the one starring on that stage.

SPILLED MILK

We went to the dining hall afterward, and I volunteered to buy the refreshments. I was balancing a tray of tall drinks when I accidentally walked smack bang into Arnie himself. Orange juice, apple juice, and milk flew in the air and splattered all over him,

ruining his outfit and making him smell like a moldy fruit bowl.

I tried to apologize, but the floor was so slippery that when I reached for Arnie he slipped and landed flat on his back with his legs in the air. Everyone gasped. There was a shocked silence. And then everyone started laughing. It was impossible not to.

I giggled, too, until I realized Arnie wasn't laughing. I imagined Dad's reaction if he heard I'd upset a dashing unicorn and realized I had to make things better.

With a wink at the crowd, I took a short run up and skidded along the damp floor, sliding through the icky sticky mess, until I came to a halt next to Arnie, who still struggling to stand up. I felt like I'd never be clean again, but it was worth it—I got a standing ovation and Arnie stopped shaking.

"Arnie and I have invented a new drink!" I declared, helping Arnie to his hooves and making him take a bow with me. "The apple-and-orange milk shake, with a dash of unicorn horn!"

And, sure enough, that's what everyone ordered for the rest of the evening.

Greetings, beloved parents,

I'm having a fabulous time here in New York, learning so many new and wonderful things. I always wondered why we unicorns have horns, and now I know—for making holes in doughnuts! Mom, I've found my happy place. It's a café that makes the best cupcakes in the world. You'd love it—except the part at the end when they bring you the check.

I also had my first taste of life as a New York superstar. During our first show, I looked out from the stage and saw hundreds of humans waving their vegetable produce in time with my performance. It was incredible. I won't be able to look at carrots in the same way again.

Dad, I think you'd be proud of me, too. I stopped a fellow unicorn from being sad yesterday. Although you'd be less impressed that it has left me smelling like moldy milk. Not dashing!

The best thing about being here is I've made some wonderful friends: a mermaid, a faun, and even a troll from Big Bad Mountain, who isn't bad at all (he is big, though!). The teachers are also lots of fun. At first I thought it was just the school principal, Madame Swirler, who loved playing hide-and-seek, but now Mr. Curtains loves it, too. He usually has some kind of bandage or plaster cast on his body, though, which makes him easy to spot.

I'll write again soon, since I know I'll have many more exciting stories about my adventures with my wonderful new friends.

Love you more than cake,
xoxo

Louie

READ ON FOR
MORE ADVENTURES
WITH LOUIE THE
UNICORN.

Looking as thrilled as a spider at a spring cleaning party, Madame Swirler lifted the microphone.

"Good morning, students." She cleared her throat, and started again. "Actually, make that "average morning," students. As some of you already know, this year is our school's fiftieth anniversary. Personally, I don't understand people's obsession with birthdays and anniversaries, but the mayor has declared that there should be a celebration. So, in honor of fifty years of the New York School of Performing Arts, we will be holding a grand performance that, for one night only, will be staged on Broadway."

Everybody cheered.

"The play we'll perform will be *The*

Handsome Prince and the Princess Pointlessly Stuck in the Tower."

There were a few cheers from the students who saw themselves as Handsome Princes, or Pointlessly Stuck Princesses.

"Now," Madame Swirler continued, "just because princes are traditionally played by humans, it doesn't mean our favorite unicorn wouldn't be great for the part." She winked at Arnie, who was sitting in the front row, preening himself.

People say Madame Swirler is mean, but they couldn't be more wrong. Look how kind that wink was. She was obviously trying to make Arnie feel better, because everyone knows who her favorite unicorn is . . . ME!